Grandfather's Pencil
and the Room of Stories

Written and Illustrated by
MICHAEL FOREMAN

Copyright © 1993 by Michael Foreman

First published in Great Britain in 1993 by Andersen Press Ltd., 20 Vauxhall Bridge Road, London SW1V
2SA. Published in Australia by Random House Australia Pty., 20 Alfred Street, Milsons Point, Sydney, NSW
2061. All rights reserved. Printed and bound in Italy by Grafiche AZ, Verona.

ISBN 0 86264 457 7

Andersen Press · London

THE boy finished the letter to his father.

He put down his pencil and climbed into bed.

HE kissed his mother goodnight.
All was quiet.
The house slept in the moonlight. The boy dreamed
in his bed. The pencil lay on the paper.

Then there was a scratchy, scribbly sound. The pencil
was writing.
"I remember," wrote the pencil, "I remember when I
first came to this house. I was in a box with friends.
We were all different colours. We were a present for
the boy."

"I REMEMBER the shop where we were bought. The shelves were full of bottles of ink and boxes of paints in sets like soldiers.

And paper – so many kinds of paper – smooth, rough, thick, thin. Papers from all over the world. Oh, the stories they told, in the night, in the dark!"

"I REMEMBER the forest where we lived before we were pencils. I was part of a very tall tree. In my dreams I still feel the sway of the treetop in the wind." In the boy's room a slight breeze ruffled the paper.

"Yes," sighed the paper, "I also remember the wind and the forest."

The pencil wrote as the paper told its tale.

"I ALSO remember when the men came and many trees were cut down. I remember the dragging of the logs and the thrilling journey down the river," said the paper.

"Ahem! Ahem! I remember that journey," said the table.
"Harum-scarum over the rapids, swinging round the bends.
I also remember the hook and chains and screaming
saw blades."

"AND then the quiet of the workshop and the loving hands that made me what I am today."

All was quiet in the room while the pencil wrote the table's tale.

"Do you remember those early days in the forest?" squeaked the door as it slowly opened. "Our hopes and dreams? Would we stay safe in the forest or travel the world? We have come a long way, but the boy has far to go."

The boy stirred in his bed. A pool of moonlight lay on the floorboards of the room.

"WE have come further than any of you," croaked the floorboards. "Long before this house was built we were part of a great ship with cream sails and a black flag.

We lived on tar and salt and loved every pitching, rolling minute of the wind in the rigging and the swish of the sea. Oh, to feel such a wind again!"

"You will!" cried the old wooden window as it flew open. The night wind whirled madly into the room.

The boy sat up, his eyes wild with excitement. The door danced on its hinges, the pencil rolled off the table and dropped into the pool of moonlight and the paper flew out of the window.

O
UT, over and beyond the city, tumbling and swooping
in the sky until it was caught and held in the top most
branches of a tree in the forest.

And these tales of the pencil, the paper, the door and the floor were torn by the wind.

BIRDS wove the tattered tales into their nests and sang the stories to their young. All the animals of the forest listened, and so the stories spread from the highest leaf to the deepest root. The stories had come home to the forest.

AND the boy? The boy who had far to go?

He grew up and sailed the oceans of the world.

WHEN he grew too old to sail he lived in a wooden house by the sea and told his stories to his grandson, Jack. At night he slept in a sea of dreams.

Then, one day, he told Jack of the night, long, long ago, when his boyhood room had filled with the night wind, and the door danced and a pencil stood on its point before it plunged into a pool of moonlight and disappeared.
"It was in your room, Jack. In your house in the city."

WHEN Jack got back to the city he rushed straight to his room.

HE lay down and peered into the cracks between the floorboards. He couldn't see anything. It was pitch black.

Jack straightened a wire coathanger and trawled up and
down between the boards. He found several things of his
own which he had lost and half forgotten. Then, finally, he
hooked out an old pencil!

He tried it on his note pad. It made a lovely, soft line. Jack wrote a 'thank you for a lovely holiday' letter to his grandfather and added:
'P.S. I have found the pencil!'

His mother came and kissed him goodnight, and he went to sleep.

The pencil lay on the paper. All was quiet.

S CRITCH, scratch. The pencil began to write…

"For many years I have lain in the dark. My companions have been a bent pin, an old gold coin and a whale bone button. Oh, the tales they told! The whale button remembered when it was part of a great whale and…"

But that is another story.